WISH UPON A
Snowflake

Illustrated by
Alison Edgson

Stripes

CONTENTS

A MAGICAL
WISHING
SNOWFLAKE

Liss Norton

It was the coldest autumn the polar bears had ever known. Snow already lay in deep drifts and the sea was frozen solid. The cold had come so early this year that there hadn't been time to gather food for the winter before the ice had arrived.

Eska shivered as a freezing wind flattened her thick white fur. "Let's have a race," the polar bear cub said. "Running will help us keep warm."

Her friend Speedy, an Arctic hare, waggled his long white ears. "OK. I'll race you to your den. One, two, three, go!"

The two friends sped away but Speedy was soon ahead. Eska ran as fast as she could, her big feet throwing up showers of powdery snow, but she couldn't catch him. By the time she reached the den, he'd already disappeared through the long entrance tunnel.

A few snowflakes drifted down from the sky and Eska stood watching them while she got her breath back. They looked like soft white feathers and were cold and tickly where they settled on her nose. "Time to go in," she said.

The den she shared with her mother was a cosy hollow under the snow. The entrance tunnel protected it from the wind and it felt warm after the bitter cold outside. Speedy was telling Mother about their race. "I got here miles ahead of Eska," he boasted.

Eska giggled. Speedy was always exaggerating. "I'll beat you one day," she warned.

"You'll need to find a magical wishing snowflake to do that." Mother laughed. "Polar bears can never outrun Arctic hares."

"What's a magical wishing snowflake?" asked Eska.

"It's a beautiful blue snowflake," explained Mother. "It doesn't melt like other snowflakes and if you hold one on your paw and make a wish, it will come true."

Eska could hardly believe her ears. "If I had one, I'd wish I could run as fast as the wind," she said. "I'd easily beat you then, Speedy!"

They all laughed. "They're very rare, Eska," said Mother. "You could search every day until the spring thaw and never find one."

"But I can try," said Eska. "Come on, Speedy. It's snowing now. Let's start looking."

The two friends hurried outside again. The snow was falling fast and they looked around eagerly, trying to spot a blue snowflake among the white ones. Eska pointed her nose to the sky while Speedy sat up on his hind legs with his whiskers twitching excitedly.

They looked for a long time but every snowflake was white.

"I don't think I'll ever find a magical wishing snowflake," Eska said glumly. She brushed a little heap of snow from Speedy's head, then shook herself and sent snowflakes flying off her fur. "I'm going to practise running instead. Even if it doesn't make me as fast as you, at least it will make me warmer!" She dashed away.

Snowflakes whirled around Eska, making it hard to see where she was going, but she ran as fast as she could. Suddenly a dark shape loomed up ahead of her. She tried to stop but she was going too fast and her paws skidded on the slippery snow. She crashed into something soft and fell over backwards.

Eska got to her feet shakily to see an

elderly brown bear lying very still on the snowy ground in front of her.

"Are you OK?" Eska asked anxiously.

The bear groaned. "I've hurt my paw. My old bones aren't as strong as they used to be."

"I'm so sorry," said Eska. She knew she shouldn't have run so fast when she could hardly see. She helped the bear up.

The bear leaned heavily on her shoulder, holding her injured foot off the ground. "Could you help me find shelter, please?" she asked. "I don't think I can walk very far."

Speedy came running up. "I heard voices," he said. "Is everything all right?"

Eska quickly explained what had happened. "We'll take you to my den," she told the brown bear. "Mother will know what to do."

"What about my sledge?" the bear asked.

Eska looked around and spotted the
wooden sledge lying on its side. Parcels
wrapped in big leaves were scattered
beside it.

"You go to the den with Eska," said
Speedy. "I'll bring your things."

Eska walked slowly beside the brown bear, helping to support her as she hobbled along. They soon reached the den and Eska guided her down the tunnel.

Mother looked up in surprise as they came inside, then she beamed at the brown bear. "Lily?" she said. "Is that you?"

"Marta!" the brown bear cried. "How wonderful!"

"You know each other?" said Eska. She knew that brown bears lived a long way off where the weather was warmer. How on earth did her mother know Lily?

"I travelled to the southern lands before you were born, Eska," said Mother. "I met Lily there and we became good friends." She helped Lily sit down. "What are you doing so far north?" she asked as she started to examine Lily's sprained paw. It looked swollen and sore.

"We brown bears realized it was going to be a hard winter because the birds flew south so early," Lily explained. "We thought you and all the other polar bears living up here might be hungry so we made up food parcels. I volunteered to bring them because I hoped I'd find you."

"How kind!" cried Mother. "We'll be very glad of some extra food. And it's lovely to see you again, Lily… But shouldn't you be hibernating now?"

"I'll hibernate when I get home," Lily replied. "Bringing food to you is much more important."

The three bears heard paws scampering down the tunnel then Speedy appeared.

"I've brought your sledge and parcels," he said. "There are millions of them!"

"Not quite that many," said Lily with a smile. Then she sighed. "I'm afraid I won't be able to deliver them to everyone now."

Eska felt hot with shame. It was her fault Lily was hurt. And now the other polar bears would have a hungry winter. Unless…

"Me and Speedy will do the deliveries for you!" she cried.

"That's a good idea, Eska," said Mother. "But you must only visit the polar bears who live near us. I don't want you going too far. And Speedy's mother will feel the same, I'm sure."

"We'll stay close," Eska promised.

Mother began to bandage Lily's paw, and Eska and Speedy ran outside. There certainly weren't *millions* of parcels, but there were lots of them, all piled high on the sledge – more than enough for all the polar bears Eska knew.

"Let's get started," she said, taking hold of the sledge's rope.

The sledge skimmed over the snow behind them as they ran along. They called at the homes of their polar bear neighbours and handed over Lily's parcels.

"Just what we need!" they said gratefully. "There's precious little food about with all this snow and ice. Please thank your mum's friend for us."

"We will," promised Eska.

It took more than an hour to visit every polar bear who lived near them and there was still a mound of parcels on the sledge when they'd finished.

"Gosh!" gasped Speedy. "There are so many parcels to deliver. I hope Lily's paw gets better soon." He and Eska hurried home.

When they returned, Lily was still sitting with Mother in the den. Her paw was neatly bandaged but there was a worried look in her eyes.

"How are you?" Eska asked. "Can you walk yet, Lily?"

"Not very well," she replied sadly.

Eska began to pass on all the messages of thanks from the polar bears but Speedy suddenly gave an excited squeal. "Eska! Your head!"

"What about it?" she asked, puzzled.

Speedy leaped from foot to foot with excitement. "I don't believe it!" he cried. "But it's true!"

"What is?" Eska couldn't understand what he meant. "What's wrong with my head?" She patted her nose and cheeks but they felt just the same as usual.

Mother looked up. "My goodness!" she gasped. "Who would have thought…?"

Eska reached up higher and felt something cold and hard on the top of her head. She picked it off and looked at it. Then her eyes grew wide. She was holding a beautiful blue twinkling snowflake.

"A magical wishing snowflake!" she breathed.

Speedy skipped around her, his ears flopping up and down. "You can make your wish now," he whooped. "Then you'll be able to run faster than the wind."

Eska shook her head. "There's something much more important to wish for." She held the snowflake on her paw and said in a loud, clear voice, "I wish Lily's paw was better."

The snowflake began to glow, then blue light poured out of it and arched across the den, making the snowy walls glitter brightly. Eska stared in wonder as the light wrapped itself around Lily's injured paw and then suddenly the snowflake vanished.

Lily moved her paw from side to side. "My paw doesn't hurt one bit!" she cried, taking off the bandage. The swelling had gone down and it looked completely better. "Thank you, Eska!" she said. "Now I can finish my deliveries."

She stood up to leave and hugged Marta. "It was lovely to see you again and to catch up with all your news."

They all went outside to say goodbye. It had stopped snowing but the sky looked heavy and white, as though it were holding a great heap of snowflakes that might tumble down at any moment.

Lily handed them each a parcel from the sledge. "Think of me when you eat them," she said. Then she hurried away across the snow, walking without even a hint of a limp.

"Goodbye," Eska called after her. "And thank you for the food!"

They waved until Lily was out of sight, then Mother went back inside.

"What a shame your wish is used up," said Speedy. "You'll never be a fast runner now."

Eska smiled. "I'm glad I made Lily better instead," she said. "And you never know – we've already found one magical snowflake. If we try hard enough, maybe we'll find another one!"

As she spoke, the snow began to fall again. She and Speedy grinned at each other.

"Let's start looking right now," Speedy said. "Bet I find one first!"

THE LOST OWL

Katy Cannon

Dear Santa,

I hope you and the elves are OK. This Christmas I would like a new bike please, as mine got broken last September when I was pretending to be a stunt rider in the woods. Thank you very much!

Love, Robin (age 9)

P.S. It would be really great if you could bring back my little brother Sam's toy owl. He lost it when we were playing in the woods last week. It's called Hooty and it's Sam's favourite thing in the world. Thanks.

tO SANtA,

PLEASE BRING MY HOOtY BACK FOR CHRIStMAS. I MISS HIM LotS.

LOVE, SAM (AGE 4)

Early on Christmas morning Robin and Sam raced downstairs, with Dad stumbling sleepily along behind them. Robin's heart thumped hard with excitement. Christmas was his favourite day of the whole year!

Robin dived for his stocking, grinning as he uncovered each new treasure inside.

"Maybe Hooty will be in one of these!" Sam shouted happily as he started ripping the paper off his gifts.

But when all the presents were opened, there was still no Hooty.

Dad gave Sam a big hug as his bottom lip started to tremble. Robin felt like crying, too. Sam had asked Santa to bring back Hooty. So *why* hadn't he?

"Come on, boys," Dad said. "I think I see more presents in the back garden…"

Robin and Sam followed Dad out. The weather was crisp and cold, with frost coating the bushes and trees. And there, leaning against the shed, were two bikes, with bows stuck to the handlebars.

"A new bike!" Robin forgot about Hooty for a moment as he dashed forwards to try out the bigger blue bike. Sam followed, looking uncertain about the small red one.

"Can we ride them right now?" Robin asked.

Dad laughed. "I think you might want to get dressed first!"

In record time both Sam and Robin were washed, dressed and wrapped up in their coats and scarves.

Robin whizzed up and down the pavement on his new bike, icy air whistling past his ears. When he arrived back at their front garden, he paused as he spotted something under the hedge. What was it? Something moving. Something alive. Something small and feathery…

"Dad!" Robin slid off his bike and kneeled down beside the hedge. "There's something here. I think it's a baby bird!"

They'd found lost baby animals in the

garden before – they lived right next to the woods. Dad always helped them find their way back or took them to the sanctuary at the local wildlife park if they were injured. But this bird didn't look like any of the others they'd found. In fact, it looked a bit like…

"Hooty!" Sam shouted as he got close. "Hooty's come back!"

The baby owl shrank away.

"Gently, Sam," Dad said, grabbing his arm. "We mustn't scare him."

"We need to find a box and a towel," Robin said, remembering how they had looked after the injured sparrow they'd found in the spring.

Dad nodded. "And I need to call Will at the sanctuary. I think our baby owl here might need some help."

Racing into the house and through to the kitchen, Robin climbed on a stool to lift down the little box they'd used for the sparrow.

Could the baby owl really be Hooty? It did look just like him. Maybe Santa had brought him to life and sent him home!

Robin ran upstairs to find a clean towel, then took the things outside to Dad.

Moving slowly, so as not to frighten the baby owl, Dad approached the hedge. He covered the bird with the towel and lifted him gently into the box.

"Right," Dad whispered. "Time to get him safely inside."

Back in the house, Dad went to call the sanctuary.

"Why does Dad need to call Will?" Sam reached across to prod the box but Robin stopped him.

"Because the baby owl needs to be looked after," Robin said. "He might be injured or sick."

"And then he can come home and live with us?" Sam's eyes shone with excitement at the idea of having Hooty back as a real-life owl.

But that was the problem, Robin realized. Hooty *wasn't* a toy owl any more. He was real. And real owls were wild creatures.

Robin wished Dad was there to explain but he was still on the phone. Besides, Robin knew *lots* about birds – they were his favourite sort of animal.

"Owls aren't meant to be kept as pets. They need to live out in the woods and the countryside where they can hunt mice and things."

Sam's face fell. "But … this owl is special. He's *my* Hooty."

"Once he's better, maybe he'll come back to visit us sometimes."

"That's not the same as having Hooty back," Sam said stubbornly.

"I know." Robin gave his little brother a hug.

Just then, Dad came back into the kitchen. "Will says we've done exactly the right thing. He's going to open the sanctuary for us first thing in the morning. I said we'd look after the owl until then."

Robin jumped up with excitement and Sam cheered. Even if they couldn't keep Hooty forever, at least they got to spend Christmas Day with him!

"Will gave me instructions," Dad said as they moved Hooty's box through to the lounge, where it was warmer. They set the box on the coffee table and all peered beneath the blanket. "I'm going to need you two boys to help me."

"What do we have to do?" Robin asked.

First Dad carefully felt along Hooty's wings and legs, to check if there were any broken bones.

"I think that wing looks different to the

other," Robin said, studying the owl.

"I think you're right," Dad agreed. "It might be broken. Which means we need to keep him in this box so he can't open it too much."

Next he felt the bird's stomach and chest. "Hmm."

"Hmm, what?" Sam asked.

"Will said that if the owl's stomach felt empty and his chest was thin, we could have a go at feeding him. What do you think? Do you want to try?"

"Yes!" Sam bounced up and down in excitement.

"What do we feed him?" Robin tried to remember what his books said that owls ate. "We don't have any mice."

"No, but we have the next best thing."

Dad tucked the blanket back over the box.
"Steak."

Dad cut the raw meat into tiny pieces
and they put it in the box for Hooty to eat.
The owl looked at it for a few moments,
then gobbled the first piece down.

"I think he likes it!" Sam said.

After Hooty had eaten, Dad moved the
box to a quiet, dark corner of the lounge
so he could rest while they ate their
Christmas dinner in the kitchen.

Robin tried to concentrate on his food,
and the cracker jokes and prizes, but all he
could think about was the poorly owl – and
how tomorrow they'd have to take him to
the sanctuary.

The next morning Will met their car at the front gates to the wildlife park and directed them past the giant Christmas tree outside, and through to the "Staff Only" area. For the whole drive, Robin had held Hooty's box very carefully, making sure the baby owl didn't get too shaken up.

Robin stared around him, taking everything in. He'd been to the wildlife park as often as he could persuade Dad to take him — it was too expensive to visit *every* week — but he'd never been allowed in this part before.

As Will held out his hand to take the box with Hooty inside it, Robin looked down to see Sam's huge, sad eyes.

"Please don't give Hooty away, Robin," Sam whispered.

"He lost his toy owl," Robin explained to Will. "We thought maybe this owl was sent by Santa to replace it."

Will crouched down so he was about the same height as Sam. "I bet you loved your toy owl very much." Sam nodded. "And I bet you only want what's best for this owl, too," Will went on. Sam nodded again, slower this time. "I can help him get well so he can go back to the woods with the other owls. Doesn't that sound good?"

"I suppose," Sam said doubtfully.

"Why don't you leave this little guy here with me, while you go and look around the wildlife park? I promise to take great care of him." Will gave them a friendly smile.

Sam didn't smile back. "OK. But then can I come back and see Hooty?"

"Absolutely," Will promised.

It was brilliant walking around the wildlife park without any other visitors there. Robin told his little brother everything he knew about the animals, with Dad chiming in occasionally.

Then, once they'd seen all the animals, Dad said it was time to go.

Sam was tired, so Dad carried him back to the sanctuary, where Will was waiting.

"How's Hooty?" Robin asked.

"He's just fine," Will assured them. "We'll have him back out in the wild in no time. And until that happens, you can come back and visit him whenever you like. Thank you for taking such good care of him."

"But—" Sam started.

"Come on, boys," Dad interrupted. They turned to go – until Will's voice stopped them.

"Oh! And you might want to take a quick look under the Christmas tree," Will said. "We had a visitor while you were looking at the animals – big guy, red coat, white beard…"

Santa!

Sam and Robin raced towards the tree.

There lay two parcels, wrapped up in shiny silver paper.

Sam ripped into his first. "It's Hooty!" he cried. "It's my real Hooty back! Santa did bring him!" He hugged the toy owl close to his chest. "I'll never lose you again, I promise."

Robin's heart felt too big for his chest. Santa had heard! Grinning, Robin reached for his own present and carefully unwrapped the paper to reveal a book about owls.

"Brilliant!" he gasped. He flipped open the first page and something fell out.

"It's a lifetime pass to the wildlife park and sanctuary," he whispered.

Santa had made their Christmas the most magical one yet!

MIDWINTER
MAGIC

Anna Wilson

Aluki the little fox was sad. The warm Arctic summer days had vanished. The sun came up only to say hello in the morning, then it quickly disappeared, leaving the land cold and dark.

Aluki ran over the frosty ground. She sniffed among the boulders, and searched by the light of the moon for her favourite pink and blue and white flowers. Where had they gone? And where had all her friends gone?

She lifted her nose to the icy night air. "Hello!" she called. "Where is everybody?"

Suddenly her large pointy ears picked

up a familiar scurrying sound.

"My friends!" she said.

There they were: the chipmunks and squirrels and skunks, hurrying to and fro among the tall pine trees.

"Found you!" Aluki cried. "Now it's my turn to hide."

"Sorry, we haven't got time," Ila the chipmunk said.

Then Aluki saw that the animals were collecting sticks and twigs and running with them to their dens and burrows. "What are you doing?" she asked, puzzled.

"Father says we have to make our winter beds," said Ila, "before the cold weather sets in."

"Why do you need winter beds?" Aluki asked.

Ila came closer. "Hasn't your mother told you? We have to go to sleep in the winter. It's too cold and dark to go outside, and there isn't enough for us to eat."

"For the *whole* winter?" Aluki said. Her voice squeaked with disbelief.

"Yes! See you in the spring!" Ila cried, scurrying away.

Aluki arrived back home, breathless and excited. "Mother! Mother! Are you getting our winter bed ready?"

Aluki's mother, Koko, was tidying the den. "What are you talking about?" she asked.

"My friends are going to sleep for the winter!" said Aluki. "It sounds very cosy. Although I might miss playing and running around," she added.

Koko smiled. "You'll have fun playing in the snow," she said. "We don't need a big winter sleep. Come here and I'll tell you why."

Aluki snuggled against her mother's warm body. "What is snow like?" she asked.

"It's magical," said Koko, nuzzling Aluki's head. "The snow changes our land – and us, too."

"I don't want to change!" said Aluki. "I like being a fox."

Koko laughed. "You'll always be a fox," she said. "But you'll change from a brown fox into a snow-white one."

"You're teasing me." Aluki frowned. She stuck out a small paw and inspected it. It was as brown as it had ever been.

Koko flicked her thick tail around the little fox and drew her close. "Haven't you noticed?" she said, nodding at her tail. "I'm starting to go white already."

Aluki gasped. "Oh, yes!"

"Now, do you want to hear the rest of my story?"

Aluki nodded enthusiastically. "Please!" she said.

"When the snow comes, many animals

go to sleep," Koko explained. "But with our white coats, we can continue to play and hunt and gather food."

"Who will I play with?" Aluki asked anxiously.

Koko licked the top of Aluki's ears. "You'll find new friends, my love," she said.

"But I don't want new friends!" Aluki exclaimed. And with that, she pushed Koko away and ran out of the den.

The little fox cried as she ran, her tears freezing into tiny icicles on her face.

Eventually she was worn out from crying and running. She stopped by the lake where she had paddled all summer. It was now thick with ice! It shone a silvery-blue under the starry Arctic sky. The dark fir trees that surrounded it were laced with frost.

Then she heard an extraordinary sound, as silver as the ice on the lake, as pure as the air and as sparkling as the stars in the sky.

Without pausing to think, Aluki sprang towards it. She pushed through the firs and stumbled over a rock, falling head first into a clearing.

"What is this?" said a deep voice.

The little fox blinked and looked around. She couldn't see where the voice had come from. Then she looked up and up, and saw a large reindeer bending over her.

"I'm s-sorry," she stammered. "I heard the noise you were making and—"

"Noise?" The reindeer snorted angrily through his enormous nostrils. "I'll have you know, little miss, that 'noise', as you call it, is the Midwinter Choir – the best choir in the Arctic."

"Who are you talking to?" said a different, softer, voice.

"See for yourself, Amaruq," the reindeer said.

Another face was pushed up close to Aluki's. This time it was a grey wolf.

"Oh, a little fox," she said. Her voice was kinder than the reindeer's, but Aluki was still afraid. "What are you doing here?" asked Amaruq.

"My name is Aluki," she answered, trying to sound brave. "I heard your noi— I mean, your singing. I thought it was beautiful – I wanted to find out where it came from."

"Well, now you know, so you can run along home," said the reindeer grumpily. "You've interrupted our rehearsal."

"Don't be so stern, Oki," said Amaruq to the reindeer. "Come and see, little fox."

Aluki followed the wolf into the clearing. Her eyes grew wide in wonder as she took in the group of animals before her. There were seals and bears and voles and lemmings and even ducks and geese. Some of the animals were smiling at her and she began to feel less scared.

"We're practising for the Midwinter Festival," Amaruq explained.

"Can I join you?" Aluki asked.

Silence hung in the air for a second. Then the entire group of animals burst out laughing.

"A fox? *Sing?*" Oki the reindeer scoffed. "Whoever heard of such nonsense?"

Aluki let out a sob and, turning her back on him, she ran off into the trees.

As she ran, she heard Amaruq the wolf calling out, "Little fox! Come back!"

But Aluki did not stop running until she had arrived home.

53

"Mother!" The little fox threw herself at Koko, panting and crying.

"What is it, my love?"

"Th-they laughed at me!" Aluki sobbed.

"There, there," Koko said. "Tell me all about it." She held her daughter close and listened while Aluki explained.

"…All I said was that I wanted to join in!" Aluki finished.

"Foxes may not be able to sing," said Koko, "but we can do something others can't."

Aluki flicked her ears. "What? What can we do?" she asked, sniffing her tears away.

"I'll tell you another story," said Koko. "Many moons ago, during the first Long Winter, our ancestors left their home in the

Big Land in the south. They stepped out of their dens and walked across the water to this place—"

"What do you mean?" Aluki interrupted. "How could we have *walked* across the water?"

"Because it had turned to ice."

"*All* the water?" asked Aluki. "Even the sea?"

"Even the sea. The Winter Festival celebrates the coming of the snow and the ice. Oki and his friends sing beautifully for the festival, it's true. But only we foxes can walk across the frozen water. Because of these," said Koko, pointing to Aluki's paws.

"Paws?" said Aluki. "Lots of creatures have paws."

"True," Koko said. "But not like ours.

We have thick fur on the pads of our paws, so we don't slip on the smooth ice."

Then Aluki remembered how the animals had laughed at her. "It's nice to know I have special paws but what good is that if no one else has? Who will I play with? I *wish* I could be in the festival."

In that instant, something light and soft and sparkling fell from the dark sky and landed on Aluki's nose.

Koko brushed the cold white speck away. "Look, Aluki! SNOW!"

The next morning, the snow had stopped falling and the land was covered in a soft sparkling blanket.

"I will go out to test my paws," Aluki said

to herself. "I will go walking on the ice."

She stepped out on to the fresh snow and found that she sank into it but that it was not cold on her paws. The fur on the pads kept her as warm as if she were running through the wildflowers in midsummer.

"Yippee!" she shouted as she ran to the lake.

When she arrived, there was no one else to be seen.

Could she do it? She hesitated and then took a deep breath and stepped out on to the ice. She took one step and then another…

It was easy! She trotted and leaped and landed perfectly.

"Wheeeeee!" she cried. She spun and whirled and jumped. "This is fun! Much more fun than singing."

"Is that so?" said a voice. Aluki whipped round to find herself face to face with Amaruq.

"I see you've got your winter coat," said the wolf.

"What? Oh!" Aluki looked down at herself and gasped. Her fur had become pure white.

Suddenly a cheer went up from the snow-topped trees and the creatures from the Midwinter Choir appeared.

"That was amazing!" said a little lemming, bouncing up and down.

"What a performance!" said a duck.

"She is rather good at ice skating, wouldn't you say, Oki?" Amaruq said.

"Harrumph," the reindeer replied.

Amaruq's smile widened. "Would you like to perform on the ice in the Winter Festival?"

"M-me?" said Aluki.

"Yes, you, little one."

Aluki swallowed hard. "You mean … I can join in after all?"

"Yes," said Amaruq. "As long as you don't sing."

Even Aluki had to laugh at that.

The night of the Winter Festival was clear and bright. The moon was full and there were so many stars it made Aluki's head spin to look at them. She stood on the edge of the lake and looked at the audience. It seemed there were as many animals gathered as there were stars in the sky. Then Aluki spotted her mother. She waved.

Oki cleared his throat and announced, "Welcome to the Midwinter Choir's performance … featuring our special guest, Aluki the dancing fox!"

The singing started, and Aluki spun and leaped and slid across the ice. No one had ever seen anything like it before. The crowd's cheers were deafening.

As the last song came to a close, Aluki finished her dance with a pirouette. The audience cheered as she took her bow.

"Did you like it?" Aluki asked, joining her mother in the crowd.

"It was magic, little daughter," said Koko, wiping a tear from her eye. "Midwinter magic!"

MISTLETOE'S ADVENTURE

Tracey Corderoy

"Mistletoe – faster!" called his big brother Bertie as the ponies chased around the snow-covered bushes.

"I'm trying!" Mistletoe called back. "Bertie! Bella! Wait!"

Mistletoe wasn't like his brother or sister, who were experts at galloping fast. His movements were graceful but slow. And that wasn't the *only* thing that was different about him…

Mistletoe's parents often told the story of how they had found him under the mistletoe when he was just a baby and had taken him in to be one of the family.

But unlike his tawny-brown brother and sister, Mistletoe had a sparkly snow-white coat. And then there was that horn in the middle of his forehead. No one knew why a pony would have such a thing but they loved him all the same. Even so, sometimes Mistletoe wished he was more like the others.

"Now, don't you go worrying about that," his mother would reply. Then she'd snuggle him close when the stars lit the sky and sing all three little ponies their favourite lullaby…

Follow the song of the river and the snowflakes dancing on the breeze. Find the star that twinkles brightest and your heart will lead you home…

Bertie and Bella had darted off through the trees, and Mistletoe found himself alone. He wondered whether he should go home but it was still early – teatime wasn't for hours.

"Hmmm…" he said. "Maybe I could go *exploring*." Yes! That was a very good idea. There were so many parts of the forest he hadn't seen yet.

It all looked so pretty, iced in white

snow, as Mistletoe set off through the trees. He crossed the stepping stones over the brook, watching his footing and thinking about the soft tippy-tap of his hooves. Why were *his* hooves so very small compared to the other ponies? And why did he always want to spin and dance, and not gallop like Bertie and Bella?

Mistletoe's head was so full of questions that he had stopped thinking about where he was going. Suddenly he stood still and looked around.

"Oh no!" cried Mistletoe. "I'm lost!"

"Lost?" came a voice from deep within the trees.

Mistletoe looked around again.

"Sorry. I didn't mean to scare you," said a creature as it skipped out lightly from behind a huge tree trunk.

"I—" Mistletoe began. But then he stopped and stared.

The silvery-white creature now standing before him looked just the same as Mistletoe. Same snow-white coat. Same bright shimmer. Same dainty feet. Even the same small horn in the middle of its forehead!

Mistletoe had never seen another pony like *himself.*

"Hi, I'm Jupiter." The little creature smiled.

Mistletoe smiled back. "I'm Mistletoe."

"Would you like to play?" Jupiter asked. "I know some really great games. Quick, follow me through the waterfall and—"

"W-wait!" cried Mistletoe. "*Through* the waterfall?"

"That's right," Jupiter replied with a nod.

Mistletoe looked at the waterfall. "I can't go through there. It's *far* too gushy and wild."

"Don't worry." Jupiter nodded. "Just watch me!" And with that, he walked right through the waterfall. A moment later he was back. And Jupiter, Mistletoe saw, wasn't even *wet*.

Mistletoe wasn't sure what to say but Jupiter smiled. "Let's go!" he said. He nudged Mistletoe towards the waterfall and they were both on the other side before he knew it.

Mistletoe looked down. "I'm still dry!" Then he looked around and his eyes grew even wider. "Oh, WOW!"

They were in the most beautiful forest

he'd ever seen. Soft, falling snowflakes shone like diamonds and the fir trees were filled with twinkling gems – emeralds, rubies, sapphires and pearls. They winked and shone as the sunlight caught them. Then Mistletoe noticed that in this magical place, his snow-white coat seemed to sparkle more than ever.

"Let's make stars," Jupiter said with a giggle.

"Make what?" asked Mistletoe. "But how? Hey – wait for me!"

Mistletoe had so many questions to ask but Jupiter had already danced off. With graceful twirls through the frosty air, he was making showers of little colourful stars tumble to the ground.

"Now *you* try," called Jupiter.

"Me?" gasped Mistletoe.

"Just do what I did," Jupiter called back with a smile.

So Mistletoe copied Jupiter. He danced and twirled and suddenly, to his surprise, *he* was making stars, too. He'd never been able to do anything like that on the other side of the waterfall. Mistletoe's heart was beating like a drum. "I never knew I could do that."

Jupiter beamed. "And I bet you've never made rainbows either, have you?"

"Rainbows?" Mistletoe shook his head.

"Giant ones." Jupiter nodded. "Come with me to Rainbow Hill and I'll show you!"

Jupiter trotted off and Mistletoe followed, making ribbons of stars the whole way. They leaped over the brook – back and forth. Then they wove in and out of the glimmering trees and across the diamond-bright snow. With each footstep Mistletoe took, he felt lighter and lighter, until at last…

"Jupiter," he cried. "Look at me! I'm not even touching the snow!" Jupiter was hovering above the ground, too.

"We're…" gasped Mistletoe.

"Yes." Jupiter nodded. "On *this* side of the waterfall we can fly!"

Mistletoe and Jupiter soared up through the sky.

"Wheee!" cried Jupiter, looping-the-loop. So Mistletoe tried it, too.

"Yippee!" Mistletoe giggled as he copied his new friend, making the world spin around. "This is FUN!"

Jupiter led them higher and finally they landed on the tallest hill. To Mistletoe, it felt as if they were standing on the top of the world.

"This is amazing," Mistletoe said.

"And that's not all." Jupiter smiled. "Watch this…"

Jupiter swished his white tail in a great twinkling arc and up in the sky…

"A rainbow!" cried Mistletoe. It was the brightest rainbow he'd ever seen.

Mistletoe gave the same sweeping arc of *his* tail and another huge rainbow appeared above the first.

"I did it!" he cried. "How is all this possible? I'm … I'm just a pony."

"Oh no," said Jupiter. "You're a *unicorn*. Just like me."

Jupiter took Mistletoe to meet his mum and dad and little unicorn brothers and sisters.

They had a tea party together with carrot cake and lemonade and fluffy marshmallows. And then it was time for some magical unicorn games.

"You'll never catch me." Mistletoe giggled as they played chase in the sky.

Eventually they grew tired and dizzy, and lay on the snow, counting the snowflakes drifting down and landing on their horns.

Mistletoe noticed that the sky wore the soft colours of sunset – lilac and peach and raspberry-pink with splashes of indigo blue. He thought about how his own family snuggled down at sunset to listen to his mother sing their favourite lullaby…

He jumped up. "Sorry," cried Mistletoe, "but I need to go. My family will be waiting for me."

"Your family?" Jupiter's mum looked curious.

"Yes." Mistletoe nodded. "There are five of us. There's me and Bertie and Bella and Mum and Dad, and I love them all so much."

Jupiter walked back to the waterfall with Mistletoe. "You will come back to visit, though?" he asked.

"Oh, yes," Mistletoe answered at once. "I've had a magical time. Thank you." Then off he went through the gushing water.

But when he was back on the other side, Mistletoe remembered that before he'd found Jupiter, he'd been very, very lost.

Shivering, he set off through the forest, hoping to find a path he knew. As he went, he hummed his mother's lullaby and the words turned in his mind…

Follow the song of the river and the snowflakes dancing on the breeze. Find the star that twinkles brightest and your heart will lead you home…

"The river!" cried Mistletoe. He listened very hard and there, soft and quiet, he could hear the trickling music of the river. He hurried towards the sound and began to follow its path. Sure enough, snowflakes began to dance past his ears on the breeze.

He went past trees glistening with frost

and filled with sleepy robins, on and on. Then suddenly he glimpsed some tangled bushes, like the ones where Bertie and Bella liked to play. Mistletoe looked up, and there it was! The twinkliest star in the sky, and—

"You're home!" cried his mother, rushing to meet him.

"Hooray!" cheered Bertie and Bella.

"We thought you were lost," his father gasped.

"I was. But then…" Mistletoe yawned. "I've had such a magical adventure."

"You can tell us all about it in the morning," his mother said.

And snuggling beneath the moon, Mistletoe slept – dreaming of rainbows and new friends and bright stars and huge tumbling waterfalls. He looked forward to playing with Jupiter again. But right now, he was glad to be home.

FIRE AND ICE

Jeanne Willis

It was winter. Overnight the first snow had begun to fall. Fox had smelled it coming and Owl had felt the frozen flakes on her wings as she flew silently above the moonlit forest. But the six little rabbits slept soundly, snuggled deep inside their burrow.

They were woken at sunrise by the badger twins. They were meant to sleep during the day but the badgers were far too excited to stay in bed.

"Wake up," barked Brother Badger, "Come and play in the snow!"

The little rabbits stirred. They had

heard about snow but they had never seen it before.

"Please can we go out and play, Mama?" they asked.

"Yes," she said. "As long as you promise to be careful."

"We promise," said the little rabbits.

One by one, they hopped out of the burrow and gazed in amazement at the glittery white blanket that covered the forest floor.

The badger twins, who were older than the rabbits, couldn't wait to tell them everything they knew about snow. Brother Badger was already making snowballs.

"Let's have a snowball fight," he said. "All you have to do is gather some snow and roll it into a ball ... like this!"

"And then?" asked Rabbit One.

"Then we throw them at each other!" said Sister Badger.

The rabbits looked confused.

"We just stand here and throw them?" asked Rabbit Two.

The badger twins laughed.

"No, we try and dodge each other," said Brother Badger. "It'll be fun!"

The rabbits began to make snowballs. They weren't as good at making them as the badgers because their paws were so small but they were much faster on their feet. They were just about to win the game when Brother Badger decided he'd had enough.

"I'm tired of playing with snowballs," he said. "Let's make a skid run."

"But we've just made a fresh pile," sighed Rabbit One. "What's a skid run?"

"Watch and learn," said Brother Badger.

The rabbits watched as the badger twins chose a straight path between the trees and stamped down the snow until it turned to ice.

"Now what?" asked Rabbit Three.

"We take a long run up and then we sliiiiide!" said Brother Badger, whooshing along the skid run on his tummy.

"Oh, I see. We take a long run up…" said Rabbit Five.

"And then we sliiiiide!" squeaked Rabbit Six as all the little rabbits took it in turns.

Brother Badger grew impatient waiting for his next turn. "I'm bored of skidding," he said.

"But it's my go," said Rabbit Four.

Brother Badger shrugged. "So? I want to make a Snow Badger."

"A *Snow* Badger?" said the little rabbits.

"It's a statue of a badger, made out of snow," explained Sister Badger.

The twins set about rolling snowballs – a big one for the body and a smaller one for the head. As they were patting them into a badger shape, the rabbits joined in. Standing on each other's shoulders, they added berries for eyes and a fir cone for a nose.

When it was finished, they stood back to

admire it but Brother Badger had already turned away. "That's enough of that," he said. "Let's make snow angels."

"Snow angels?" wondered the rabbits.

The badger twins lay on their backs in the snow and showed the little rabbits what to do. All six of them lay down and they were just about to make their own snow angels when they heard a loud flapping sound in the sky.

"It's a dragon!" Brother Badger cried. "My grandpa met a dragon once and he said they can't be trusted. Run for your lives!"

The rabbits scattered in fright and, as they lay quivering in the bushes with the badger twins, the dragon landed in the snow with a thump. It was only a baby but

they didn't know that – it was much bigger
than they were and it had very sharp teeth.

The dragon looked around and sniffed
the air with his long, scaly snout.

"Is he going to eat us?" whispered Rabbit
One.

"Mama will be furious," squeaked Rabbit
Two.

But they needn't have worried. To their
surprise, the dragon sat down and began to
sob. "Where have you all gone? I'm lonely!
Please let me play with you."

"Don't answer him," muttered Brother Badger. "It's a trick!"

Just then the dragon spotted the Snow Badger and went over to take a closer look.

"It's beautiful," he said. "Please will you help me make a Snow Dragon?"

Suddenly he gave a thunderous sneeze and flames shot out of his mouth and nose, melting the Snow Badger.

"Whoops!" spluttered the dragon.

Brother Badger was so angry he forgot to be afraid and came out of his hiding place.

"You've spoiled it," he said. "You can't play with us. Go away!"

"I don't think he meant any harm," said Rabbit Three.

By now the dragon had seen the skid run and his eyes lit up. He ran on the spot, flapped his leathery wings and with a loud whoop, he skidded all the way to the end.

"Wheeeee! Please come and skid with me," he said. But as he spoke, he sneezed again and his fiery breath melted the ice right down to the grass.

"Now look what you've done!" said Brother Badger.

"Sorry, I didn't mean to," said the dragon. "I have a flaming cold."

"Sorry isn't good enough – you're ruining winter," said Brother Badger. "Leave us alone!"

The dragon sniffed sadly and, dragging his spiky tail behind him, he wandered back to his cave.

Rabbit One turned to Rabbit Two and whispered in her ear, "I feel sorry for the dragon, don't you?"

Rabbit Two nodded. "Brother Badger was mean to him," she said.

But Brother Badger overheard. "I wasn't being mean, I was being *sensible*," he said. "Grandpa said dragons are dangerous and you promised your mama you'd be careful."

The rabbits remembered their promise.

"You're right. Mama will be wondering where we are," said Rabbit Three.

"We should go home," agreed Rabbit Four.

Brother Badger rolled his eyes. "You're no fun," he said. "Don't you want to go ice skating?"

The little rabbits didn't know what to say. They wanted to stay and play but it was getting dark and they were very tired. Luckily for them, Sister Badger was feeling drowsy, too.

"Why don't we all go and have some sleep?" she yawned. "We can skate in the morning. The ice won't have melted if we get up before sunrise."

"Meet us by the pond an hour before dawn," Brother Badger instructed the rabbits. "And don't tell your mama about the dragon or she'll tell *our* mama and no one will be allowed out to play."

"We won't," said the little rabbits. And in a flash of powder-puff tails, they hurried home.

It was still dark when the six little rabbits woke up. They had not told their mama about the dragon, so when they asked if they could go out to play, she let them.

"Just promise me you'll be careful," Mama said.

"We promise," they said.

They scampered off to the frozen pond under the stars. When they arrived, the badger twins were already waiting for them.

"Quick," said Brother Badger. "Last one on the ice is a ninny!"

The rabbits had never been skating before. They stood on the snowy bank and tested the ice with their toes.

"Is it dangerous?" asked Rabbit One.

"What if we fall?" said Rabbit Two.

Brother Badger laughed. "It's easy," he said. "Follow me!"

He stepped boldly on to the ice and skated off, but the rabbits didn't move.

"I'm not sure…" said Rabbit Three.

"I'll hold your paw," said Rabbit Four

"But what if Brother Badger bumps into us?" said Rabbit Five.

They watched as he showed off on the ice, doing spins and jumps and twirls.

"What are we waiting for? Come on!" said Rabbit Six. He stepped towards the edge and lifted up a paw.

Suddenly there was a loud crack.

"Oh no!" gasped Sister Badger as she looked across the pond to where her brother had been. "Brother Badger has fallen through the ice!"

Sister Badger raced towards the hole while the six little rabbits ran up and down the bank panicking.

"Paws and whiskers! Somebody do something!" they all cried.

"Where are you, Brother?" called Sister Badger.

Brother Badger bobbed back up through the hole, kicking and scrabbling as he tried to climb out. But the ice was too slippery for him to grip.

"Help!" he cried. "Help!"

The ice began to crack near Sister Badger's feet. She skated backwards to where the ice was thicker, lay down and tried to grab her brother's paw.

"I can't reach!" she wailed.

The rabbits looked at each other in dismay.

"If Sister Badger can't reach him, nor

can we," said Rabbit One. "Our arms are too short."

"A tree has long arms," said Rabbit Three. He ran off to find a branch and threw it as hard as he could to Sister Badger. "Tell Brother Badger to hold on to it!" he shouted.

Sister Badger caught the branch as it skidded across the ice and held it out to Brother Badger. He held on tight but when she tried to pull him out, he was too heavy.

"Help me!" she cried.

"We're coming!" called Rabbit One.

The six little rabbits grabbed each other round the waist and skated across the pond in a line, trying not to fall over. When they reached Sister Badger, Rabbit One held on to her and they all pulled and heaved.

But Brother Badger was even heavier now that his fur was wet and they couldn't haul him out.

"If only the sun would melt the ice," said Rabbit Two.

"There *is* no sun. It hasn't risen yet," said Rabbit Three.

Just then, Rabbit Four had a brilliant idea. "Fire melts ice," she said. "The dragon has fire!"

"Let's run and fetch him," said Rabbit
Five.

While Sister Badger stayed with her
brother and begged him not to let go of the
branch, the rabbits ran through the forest
to find the dragon. The deeper they went,
the darker it got.

"We'll never find him," said Rabbit Six.

"Listen … I hear snoring," said Rabbit
One. "Follow that snore."

Finally they found the dragon fast asleep
in his cave.

"Wake up, Dragon!" said Rabbit Two.
"Brother Badger has fallen through the
ice. We need your help! You're the only
one who can save him!"

"Me?" said the dragon.

As the rabbits talked over each other,

trying to explain what had happened, the dragon sprang off his bed of leaves.

"Climb on to my back," he said. "There's no time to lose."

The rabbits clung on tight as the dragon flew over the snowy treetops.

"There's the pond," shouted Rabbit Three.

The dragon landed on the bank with a bump and the rabbits tumbled off.

"Stand back, Sister Badger!" roared the dragon. "I can feel a big sneeze coming on…"

He took a deep breath and with a deafening "Aaa-tish-ooo!" he blasted the ice with a red-hot sneeze. Ribbons of flames shot from his nostrils as he sneezed and he sneezed until his fire had melted a strip of ice stretching from the hole where Brother Badger was trapped all the way back to the bank. It was just wide enough for Brother Badger to swim to safety.

"Keep swimming!" shouted Sister Badger as her brother made his way to the bank.

When he reached them, the rabbits helped Sister Badger and the dragon to pull out Brother Badger and there he stood, soaked and shivering and looking very sorry for himself indeed.

"I'm f-f-f-freezing," he said.

Without a moment's hesitation, the dragon scorched a little circle on the ground, covered it with branches and huffed on them to make a blazing fire.

While Brother Badger warmed up by the fire, the others all huddled round it and roasted chestnuts they had gathered from the forest floor.

Finally, after he had stopped shivering, Brother Badger realized that he owed someone a huge apology.

"I'm sorry I wouldn't let you play with us, Dragon," he said. "Grandpa was wrong. You are kind, gentle and a good friend. Thank you for saving me. Now I can go skiing!"

The six little rabbits had never been skiing. "Can we come?" they asked.

"Of course," he said.

Dragon held his breath. "Can I come?" he asked. "I'll try not to sneeze."

And this time, Brother Badger said, "YES!"

THE BLACK
SQUIRREL

Holly Webb

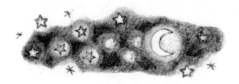

"There!" Lucy pushed the catch, and the bird feeder opened up at last.

"Well done — we needed your small fingers for that. Hold it tight for me."

Lucy's mum tipped up the bag of seed and it went rattling into the tube.

The people who had lived in their new house before them had left the bird feeder behind, but it was empty. As soon as Lucy and her mum had spotted the flock of sparrows that kept arguing in the hedge, they'd decided to pop down to the pet shop for some birdseed.

"Do you think if we sat on the bench, really still, the birds would come to the feeder?" Lucy asked.

"We could try, couldn't we?" They crept over to the bench and Lucy sat as still as she could. She felt like a spy or maybe a detective on a stakeout. The September sun was warm on her shoulders as she watched the birds fluttering in the bushes.

"Oh, look, Lucy, a butterfly!" Lucy's mum pointed to a tiny blue butterfly that spiralled around them and over the fence to next door.

Then she looked down at Lucy. "Are you glad we moved?"

"I love it that we've got a garden." When they lived in the flat, Mum had always taken Lucy to the park, but now they had their own space. The street was quiet enough to ride her bike in, too, and there were other children close by – she'd heard them playing. Suddenly Lucy spotted a movement down by the big tree at the end of the garden. "Look! There's something hopping about."

"A blackbird?" Mum said, frowning. "No, it's a squirrel!"

"Squirrels in *our* garden?" Lucy bounced a little, and then remembered they needed to keep still.

Mum laughed. "I bet he'll be at that

bird feeder, too – squirrels are so clever."

"Ooooh, Mum, he's coming closer." Lucy blinked in surprise as the squirrel began to scurry down the long, narrow lawn. "Look! He's a funny colour!"

Mum nodded. "I've never seen a squirrel like that before."

The squirrel paused in the middle of the grass, looking around cautiously, his bushy tail twitching. He wasn't grey-brown like the squirrels Lucy had seen at the park, he was a rich black all over, with round, dark eyes.

"He's beautiful! Do you think he's really rare?"

"I think he must be. I wonder if I can get a photo?" Mum edged her phone out of her pocket, trying not to make any sudden movements that might scare the squirrel away. "There!"

The squirrel's neat little round ears flickered as he heard the click of the camera and Lucy held her breath, but he didn't run away. Instead he darted over the grass towards the bird feeder and began to shimmy up the metal pole. Then he hung there, eyeing the swinging tube with the seeds in. He even leaned out to peer at it, but then he grabbed on to the pole again.

Lucy pressed her hand over her mouth, trying not to laugh. He was definitely trying to work out how to get to the seeds but the feeder hung on an arm at the top of the pole and he just couldn't reach it.

"I think that's why the feeder's on a pole," Mum whispered. "To stop squirrels getting at it."

"Why? I want to feed him, he's so cute."

"I know, but lots of people get annoyed with squirrels eating the seeds before the birds get any."

Lucy supposed that made sense – but the squirrel was so funny. He was whirling his tail about and stretching as far as he could. Then he suddenly launched himself from the pole, leaping sideways, and grabbed on to the feeder. Lucy gasped, watching it swing around as he clung on. As the feeder slowed down, the squirrel started to nibble at the seeds and nuts through the wire, wriggling about and digging his claws in. Then he seemed to notice Lucy and her mum. He stared at them for a moment, took one more bite and then leaped down on to the grass and back to the tree at the bottom of the garden.

Lucy hurried out into the garden, wishing she'd put her coat on. Now that it was October, the weather seemed to have jumped from summer straight to chilly autumn. She unhooked the bird feeder and opened the bag of seeds. They'd bought another squirrel-proof bird feeder and kept the old one for Shadow – that was the name Lucy had decided on for the black squirrel. Shadow was now working on the squirrel-proof one, as well. Lucy reckoned he thought it was a challenge. He'd tried all sorts of ways to get at it – he'd even learned to hold on to the pole with his back paws and reach out to the feeder with his front ones, but it didn't work. There were other squirrels in the garden sometimes, too, but Shadow was Lucy's favourite.

As she tipped up the birdseed, Lucy caught a glimpse of something dark running along the top of the wall. She turned, very slowly, and saw Shadow sitting there – obviously waiting for her to finish. He put his head on one side as he saw her watching, but he didn't flip his tail about or make the funny yapping noise that Lucy had heard the squirrels using. It was an alarm call, she was pretty sure. They'd yapped to each other when Gracie, the gorgeous cat from next door, was stalking along the wall. Lucy tipped in the birdseed, still with one eye on Shadow then clicked it closed.

"I've got something for you," she whispered, digging her hand in her pocket. "The man in the pet shop said squirrels love them." She sat down on the grass, very slowly. She could feel the damp seeping into her jeans but she didn't mind. "Here," she whispered, holding out a handful of monkey nuts. The pet shop owner had explained that they were like peanuts, except they hadn't had the cases taken off.

The squirrel leaned forwards a little, peering at Lucy's hand. He ran up and down the wall, then all of a sudden he seemed to make a decision. He leaped on to the grass and bounded towards Lucy in little bursts. When he was no more than a metre away, he sat back on his haunches and stared at her – and the food.

Lucy shook her hand a little so the nuts rattled, then picked one out. She threw it very gently so that it landed between her and the squirrel. He glared at it suspiciously, the black fluff of his tail twitching. But it was only one little jump away...

He bounced forwards and grabbed it, seizing the nut between his tiny black paws. Then he darted away up the garden. He was probably going to take the nut somewhere safe to eat, Lucy thought. Or maybe he was already storing up nuts for the winter? She knew that squirrels were known for burying food and forgetting where they'd put it but she wasn't sure it was cold enough for that yet.

Over the next few weeks, Shadow came closer and closer to Lucy each time she fed him. He always seemed to be around after school and she showed him off to her friend Lara, when she came for tea. Lara had a pet hamster and Lucy loved to hold him, but she and Lara agreed that an almost-pet squirrel was much more exciting. They watched him bound back up the tree at the end of the garden and Lara peered up into the branches.

"Is that a bird's nest?" she asked, pointing to a ball of sticks and leaves high up in the tree.

Lucy shook her head. "No, Shadow's building it. It's his winter nest. I looked it up online – it's called a drey. It's all lined with moss and feathers and then the squirrels use their tails like a fluffy blanket. I wish I could see him, all curled up in there…"

Lucy banged the kitchen door behind her and kicked off her boots. Her mum looked up at her in surprise. "What's the matter? Oh, Lucy, your hands are blue! It's freezing today. I wouldn't be surprised if we had snow soon. We might have a white Christmas!"

"Shadow's not there again! I haven't seen him in days! In fact…" Lucy shook her head, frowning worriedly. "Mum, it's been nearly two weeks." Lucy slumped down at the kitchen table. "What if he's sick? Or one of the cats caught him? I've seen Gracie chasing squirrels…"

Her mum reached out to hug her. "Lucy, I'm sure it's OK. Gracie never actually catches them, does she?"

Lucy wrinkled her nose. "Not yet…"

"Maybe Shadow's just sleeping through the winter?"

"Squirrels don't hibernate, Mum. I looked it up."

"I know, but that website said they can sleep for days sometimes. They only nip out briefly when they need to access their food stores. Shadow must have food buried all over the place – think how many peanuts you've given him!"

"Are you sure?"

But Lucy didn't wait for an answer – she raced down the garden in her socks with a little pile of monkey nuts, which she left at the bottom of the tree trunk. She peered up at the drey. "I hope you're wrapped up in your tail blanket," she whispered into the dark branches. "Mum says it's going to snow…"

Lucy huddled further under her duvet. It was colder than ever and her nose felt icy. She was enjoying the feeling of knowing she didn't have to hurry to get up now it was the Christmas holidays. She wondered what time it was – her bedroom was quite light. Lucy peered out over the edge of her duvet. It was *very* light. Almost as if…

She squeaked and scrambled out of bed. Yes! There was a thick layer of snow over the garden and the dark tree had turned lacy white. That meant Shadow's drey would be snow-covered, too, like a little igloo. She could just see it – a little snowy lump at the crook of the branches. Lucy shivered, wondering if Shadow was cold.

And then she saw him. Darting along

a snow-covered branch, a little black figure against the sparkling whiteness. Lucy dashed downstairs, grabbing her fleece on the way and hopping about as she dragged on her boots. She filled her pockets with monkey nuts and then took a deep breath before she opened the door – if she raced out like she wanted to, she'd scare Shadow away.

Instead she crept outside, a few nuts in her hand, the snow squeaking and crunching under her boots. The black squirrel sprang down on to the grass and gazed at her, one paw held up.

Lucy crouched down, holding out a nut, and Shadow padded delicately towards her, so light that he could scamper over the thin, frozen crust of the snow.

"Hello..." Lucy whispered.

The black squirrel gazed back at her. Then as he leaned in to take the nut, he rested one tiny dark paw against Lucy's hand, just for a second, as if he was saying thank you.

HELPFUL
BARNABAS

Michael Broad

As the late autumn wind whistled through the forest, Barnabas the black bear cub was chasing dried leaves, leaping up to catch them as they swirled around and fluttered away. He was meant to be helping his mum collect them but Barnabas loved to play more than anything else in the world. Everything he did became a game!

"It will soon be time to hibernate and there's still so much to do," said his mum as she gathered up the last of the leaves and stuffed them into their winter mattresses. "Now our bedding's ready, there's just enough time to prepare the cave for tomorrow's feast."

"I want to help!" Barnabas said excitedly and hitched a ride on the plump mattresses as his mum dragged them back into their cave. He then climbed up on to the table as she set out jars of jam and honey and a sack of flour.

"There's no time for games," said Mum, when Barnabas dipped his paw in the flour and puffed on it to make a cloud. He then stacked the jars like building blocks, which his mum only just managed to catch as the colourful tower came tumbling down.

"Oops!" said Barnabas.

"Why don't you see if your friends want to play?" said Mum, lifting Barnabas off the table so she could set to work making her famous jam tarts and honey biscuits. "Tomorrow may be the last time we'll see anyone until spring, so make the most of the time you have left."

"But I wanted to help bake something for the forest feast."

"Maybe next year," said Mum, and kissed him on the nose.

Barnabas did as he was told and went into the forest to find his friends, but he wasn't his usual cheerful self. "I wish I could make something for the forest feast," he said, kicking up the leaves as he went.

"Watch where you're kicking, Barnabas!"

said a familiar voice at his feet.

Barnabas looked down to see his friend Chuck the chipmunk.

"What are you doing, Chuck?" asked Barnabas.

"My dad sent me out to find acorns," said Chuck, holding up his basket, which was mostly empty, and treading carefully as he looked on the ground. "But there aren't many around so late in the year."

Barnabas spotted a few acorns close by and squatted down to help, but he wasn't very good at picking them up because his paws were too big.

"Don't worry, there's a bit of a knack to it," said Chuck, picking them up easily and tossing them into the basket. "It's time for me to go home anyway. My dad wants me to help with baking bread for the forest feast."

"I wish I could help," said Barnabas, kicking another pile of leaves as they set off.

"You can help by kicking up more leaves," said Chuck, darting around in his friend's footsteps and filling his basket.

"That's just playing," sighed Barnabas, as Chuck continued to hop and dance around him. But he loved to kick leaves, so he did it all the way to the chipmunk's burrow as they sang a cheerful song about gathering acorns.

Barnabas said goodbye and stomped on through the woods. Soon he came to a clearing with a massive old oak tree.

"Mind my mushrooms, Barnabas!" said a familiar voice.

Barnabas jumped and then looked round to see his friend Sookie the skunk. She was gazing sadly at his feet.

"What are you doing?" asked Barnabas. He followed her gaze and saw several squashed mushrooms, where he'd accidentally stomped them into the ground.

"Mum sent me off to find mushrooms," said Sookie, pointing to her basket. "But they're all really small. I'm not sure they'll be any good."

"Can I help?" asked Barnabas. He hurried around looking for more of the little mushrooms to pick. But he was so clumsy that he squashed more than he picked and there weren't very many around to begin with.

Sookie looked at the mushrooms and her basket, then at Barnabas and the oak tree.

"Would you mind climbing up the tree?" she said.

"Huh?" said Barnabas. "That's not helping. That's playing."

"It would help me very much," said Sookie. She pointed up at the lumpy old tree that had fat blooms of fungus growing around its trunk and on the thick branches above them.

Barnabas didn't need to be asked twice. Climbing trees was one of his favourite things to do. But he was pretty sure Sookie

only asked him so he
wouldn't be in the way
and squash any more
mushrooms. She
carried on filling
her basket below
while they chatted
about the coming winter and the forest feast.

"My mum's making sweet treats with
jam and honey," said Barnabas, drooling at
the thought of them. "And Chuck and his
dad are baking bread."

"My mum is making pies, so I have to go
home now to help," said Sookie.

Barnabas climbed back down the tree,
swung on the lowest branch and landed
beside his friend as she pulled a cloth across
her basket.

"See you tomorrow, then!" they said together, and Barnabas headed down to the river. The bear cub charged down the bank and began splashing in the water. He was having so much fun and making so much noise, he didn't even notice he had company.

"Stop splashing, Barnabas!" said a familiar voice nearby.

Barnabas looked up to see his friend Raz the raccoon, who was waving at him from a large rock in the middle of the shallow stream.

"What are you doing, Raz?" asked Barnabas, clambering up on to the rock.

"Fishing," said Raz, lifting up his basket. "But I haven't caught a single one yet!"

"Sorry for splashing. I must have scared them all away," said Barnabas. "Is there anything I can do to help?"

Raz looked Barnabas up and down and scratched his chin.

"You can splash some more if you want?"

"But that's just playing," said Barnabas. "And it scares off the fish."

"Not if you're over there," said Raz, pointing a short distance away.

The two friends jumped into the water and Barnabas headed upstream. There he started kicking and splashing and having a brilliant time, cheered on by his friend, who finally seemed to be having some luck.

By the time the two friends left the
river and headed back into the woods the
basket was full of fish.

"That was great fun!" said Barnabas.

"It wasn't until you came along," said
Raz.

Barnabas asked his friend what his
family were bringing to the forest feast.

"They're making a stew," said Raz. "I
have to go back and help."

"I'll see you there," said Barnabas, and
he headed for home, too.

The next day, as Barnabas's mum prepared
to host the forest feast, she noticed that
Barnabas wasn't joining in with his usual
fun and games.

"What's wrong?" she asked, sitting down beside him.

"I wanted to bring something to the feast so I tried to help my friends," he said. "But I wasn't helpful at all and just kept getting in the way."

"I'm sure that's not true," said Mum. "I wish I'd asked you to help me with my baking instead of sending you off to play. I could have used a little helper."

"Really?" said Barnabas.

"And now it would really help me if you could set the table before all our friends arrive."

Barnabas didn't have to be asked twice. He jumped up and raced around the table, singing to himself about plates and cups and cutlery. There were so many pieces for so many guests that he made a game out of it.

"What a wonderful job you've done," said Mum.

The guests soon arrived with platters and plates and huge pots with lids on. Everyone gathered round as the food was laid out. The raccoons placed their steaming stew in the middle of the table. The skunks set their golden pies down and the chipmunks filled baskets with crusty loaves of bread. Barnabas set out the jam tarts and honey biscuits, and when everyone was seated, his mum stood up to make a toast.

"I would like to welcome all our good friends to this year's forest feast," she said. "And to thank you for bringing this wonderful food to the table. I know it's difficult finding anything to eat as winter draws close. Everyone has worked very hard to put this feast together."

"Especially Barnabas," said Chuck.

Sookie and Raz nodded in agreement.

"Me?" said Barnabas. "I thought I just played and got in the way."

"But you kicked away all the autumn leaves and that meant I could fill a whole basket with acorns for Dad's acorn bread!" said Chuck. He patted one of the many large loaves laid out along the table. "I had found hardly any acorns before you came along."

"And you climbed up that big old oak tree, knocking off all the large blooms of tree fungus for me," said Sookie. She pointed to the plates of pies her family had made from the mushrooms. "Before you arrived

I had only found a few small mushrooms."

"And if you hadn't shown up at the river and scared the fish in my direction, we'd be having hot-water soup," said Raz. He lifted the lid from one of the steaming clay pots, filling the air with lovely fishy smells. "Because of your help we can all enjoy a delicious fish stew."

Barnabas didn't know what to say, so he looked around at his friends and gave a huge smile.

"Here's to Barnabas!" his mum said. "The most *helpful* playful bear!"

"To Barnabas!" everyone cheered, then began tucking into their delicious food.

Chuck, Sookie and Raz each heaped extra large portions of soup, pie and bread on to their friend's plate, and Barnabas

was sure the food tasted better than ever.
They even insisted that he got the last jam
tart and the last honey biscuit!

THE TROUBLE WITH TIBBLES

Lucy Courtenay

Tibbles turned round on the mat outside the back door a few times and looked at Martha. She was wearing her cosy Christmas pyjamas, the ones Tibbles liked to sit on the moment they came out of the tumble dryer.

"Come inside, Tibbles," Martha said. "I'm getting cold."

Tibbles waved his stripey tail and rubbed his ears against her outstretched fingers. The house was always cosy on Christmas Eve and his family gave him fresh tuna for dinner. Father Christmas usually left him a treat as well… The thought of food made

Tibbles hungry but he could hear rustling in the garden and he wanted to go hunting. He looked over his shoulder, wondering what to do.

"Come on, Tibbles!" said Martha, stamping her feet and shivering.

This is a difficult decision, thought Tibbles. *Don't rush me.* He sat on the mat so that his tummy spilled over his paws, keeping his toes nice and toasty while he thought about things. The rustling behind him stopped.

"Shut the door, Martha!" Mum shouted. "You're letting in the cold air."

"Tibbles won't come in!" Martha called back.

"He can use the cat flap!"

"I think he's too fat for the cat flap, Mum."

How rude, thought Tibbles.

"He'll be fine," Mum called. "Come on, I need some help setting out the Christmas stockings before bed."

Martha looked at Tibbles. Tibbles looked at Martha.

"Coming," Martha said.

As soon as Martha shut the door, Tibbles decided he wanted to be inside after all. He thought about the bright red baubles dangling from the Christmas tree, at just the right height for him to play with. And there was wrapping paper he could tear with his claws and rolls of sticky tape he could chase along the carpet. He was still hungry, too. Starving, in fact. He hadn't eaten for at least an hour.

The cold air blew through Tibbles's thick tabby fur and he scratched at the door once more, mewing feebly.

Dad flung open the door. "Are you coming in this time, Tibbles?" he said.

But just at that moment the rustling started again from somewhere deep in the garden. A cheeky mouse, Tibbles was sure of it. He'd teach it a lesson. Perhaps he could even catch it for Mum – as a Christmas present. He spun round and rushed after the sound.

Behind him the door closed again but Tibbles didn't notice. He was too busy hunting the mouse.

After several minutes of stalking up and down the lawn, he spotted two beady black eyes watching him from underneath some leaves. He put his ears back and flattened his tummy against the ground. It didn't make him very flat at all. He waggled his bottom and sprang into the leaves.

Got you! thought Tibbles.

But the mouse had gone.

The mouse was harder to catch than Tibbles expected. It ran into a hole beneath the shed, where he couldn't reach it. Tibbles sat down breathlessly and washed his ears and his fat, furry belly. He used to be able to get under the shed with no trouble at all.

Tibbles's tummy made an extra-loud rumbling noise and he decided to go inside and ask for his supper.

He padded over to the back door.

"Meow," he said impatiently.

He could see the lights on the Christmas tree twinkling through the French windows, flashing pink and green and blue. Tibbles listened for the usual sounds his humans made but it was strangely quiet.

"Meow?" he said a little louder.

No one answered.

Tibbles didn't like the cat flap but it seemed like he didn't have much choice.

The cat flap opened easily enough, but then it swung back suddenly and smacked him on the nose. Tibbles gave his crumpled whiskers a quick wash and tried again. His head went through. His right paw went next and then his left. Tibbles pushed off the doormat with his back legs…

And stopped. His tummy didn't fit.

Tibbles scrabbled with his back legs. He huffed and puffed. But it was no good. He couldn't get his tummy through the flap.

My humans must have made it smaller, he thought.

Tibbles backed out again with difficulty. He washed his tail for a moment as he thought about what to do next. Then he scrambled up the fence by the back door and jumped on to a windowsill.

"Meow?" he called.

Nothing.

Tibbles started feeling anxious. He leaped up to a piece of guttering, which creaked and bent underneath him. With some effort, he clambered up and sat down on the roof.

No one cares that I'm cold or hungry, he thought sadly. *These humans don't deserve me.*

Snuggling up to the chimney bricks, he closed his eyes and dreamed of putting a mouse on Mum's pillow.

It was the thud that woke him up.

"Whoa there, Dancer. Steady now, Vixen," said a deep voice.

Tibbles peered round the chimney at the sleigh looming over him. A burst of strange whinnying made him flatten his ears and the deep voice laughed.

"Ho, ho, ho! I won't forget your carrot, Comet. Now then…"

There was a puffing sound and a scraping noise. It reminded Tibbles of the noise he'd made earlier, trying to squeeze through his cat flap.

"They've made this chimney smaller!" panted the voice.

I know how you feel, thought Tibbles.

"Ah!" said the voice after a few more wriggles. "There we go!"

There was a whooshing noise and then silence. Tibbles eyed the row of hooves standing on the roof and gazed at the soft red velvet lining of the sleigh. It looked just like Martha's pyjamas.

He padded out from his hiding place. One of the hooved creatures gazed at him with bright coal-black eyes as Tibbles scrambled into the sleigh.

The red velvet lining wasn't just soft, but squashy, too. There were white furry blankets and cushions, and several hot-water bottles decorated with knitted Christmas trees. Tibbles kneaded a hot-water bottle and shredded the corner of a furry blanket, then curled himself up right in the middle of all the cushions and fell fast asleep.

Tibbles dreamed about fat mice scurrying straight into his mouth. He dreamed of large Christmas baubles, long pieces of tinsel, fresh tuna and humans who opened doors for him all day long.

He had no idea how long he'd been asleep when someone sat on him. Hard. He tried to yowl but he got a mouthful of velvet and it came out as a squeak. He tried to move but he was squashed too flat.

This was not good.

"The cushions are lumpier than usual," said the deep voice.

Tibbles squirmed. The person sitting on him didn't notice.

"Come, Dasher! Come, Dancer! Now,

Prancer and Vixen!"

The sleigh shifted to the sound of jingling bells.

Tibbles wriggled, heaved in as much breath as he could, flexed his paws and…

"On, Comet, on, Cupid, on, Donner and—"

"MEOW!" roared Tibbles, sinking his claws into the red velvet bottom.

"OW!" roared the voice.

The bottom flew upwards.

Gasping for breath, Tibbles saw a flash of night sky overhead. The sleigh jerked and tipped from side to side. And all of a sudden, it appeared to be flying.

"MEOW!" he bellowed in fright, racing round the sleigh as the world fell away beneath him.

"It's a cat!" cried the deep voice. "There's

a cat in my sleigh! Whoa there, Blitzen,
steady now, Prancer…"

The sleigh swooped and dipped and
turned in crazy circles.

What's happening? Tibbles thought.
Where is my house? Where is my chimney?
Where are my humans?

"MEOW!" Tibbles roared again.

He glimpsed his house over the gilded edge of the sleigh. He could picture his toys and his food bowl decorated with fish and his bed by the fire.

Gathering all of his courage, Tibbles jumped. The night air whistled through his fur. He scrabbled at the air with his claws, twisting in the wind. He stretched out his legs. He gazed at the rooftop speeding towards him and the black chimney hole. It looked so small. Smaller even than his cat flap.

Tibbles sucked in his tummy as far as it would go.

Whumph!

He felt the scrape of bricks on his sides and then before he knew it he had landed feet first in a cloud of soot and ash. He sat, panting and winded, and looked around.

The tree was there … and the presents. The wrapping paper and the sticky tape. A glass of half-finished wine and the nibbled end of a carrot. The clock ticked quietly on the mantelpiece, like it had all the time in the world.

Tibbles examined his filthy coat. He'd never felt so hungry but food would have to wait.

I have standards, he thought to himself.

And so he washed his tail all down one side and then all down the other. He licked his paws. He scrubbed at his ears. Only when he was clean did he head into the kitchen, where he gobbled up the fresh tuna in his bowl and drank every last drop of his water. Then, when he was finished, he coughed up a splendid hairball right in the middle of the kitchen floor.

He padded back to the Christmas tree and took a deep breath of its clean pine scent. A little packet in the shape of a fish dangled on the lowest branch. Cat treats from Father Christmas.

I definitely need a treat, thought Tibbles.

He ripped open the packet with his claws and finished the lot. Finally he eyed the red baubles swinging gently in the branches and patted them until they dropped off the tree and broke on the carpet.

Home, thought Tibbles happily as he settled down in his bed.

Home, sweet home.

THE
UNEXPECTED
VISITOR

Linda Chapman

Esme Browne sat at the kitchen table making shapes using leftover bits of pastry while her dad made mince pies.

"By the time Mum gets in tonight," Dad said, "I'd like to have all the decorations up. Your mum's been so busy, I want to give her a surprise."

Esme nodded. Her mum and dad were vets, and her mum had been out on call every night that week.

"Two weeks from now it'll be Christmas Day!" she said.

"Have you written your Christmas list?"

her dad asked.

"I don't need to." Esme pushed her long dark ponytail over her shoulder. "You know there's only one thing I want!" She gave her dad a hopeful look. "Pleeeeease can we get a dog?"

Her dad sighed. "Esme, we've talked about this. Mum and I are so busy taking care of other people's animals, we don't have time to look after a dog of our own."

"But Alex and I will look after it," said Esme. "We've read tons of dog care books. We'd do everything!" She saw her dad open his mouth to speak but she rushed on. She and her brother had it all figured out. "We could get a rescue dog – an older dog wouldn't need so much attention. And when we're at school it could stay in a crate at the

surgery, like Tosca." Tosca belonged to Sue,
the receptionist at her parents' vet practice.

Mr Browne smiled. "You really have
thought it all through, haven't you?"

"Yes!" exclaimed Esme.

"Well, maybe one day we can but
not this Christmas, sweetheart." Her dad
brushed the pastry off his hands. "Now,
time to start decorating the house. Can
you and Alex sort out the lounge?"

The excitement Esme had been feeling at the thought of Christmas had faded a bit, now she knew they definitely weren't getting a dog. She went through to the lounge. Alex's eyes were glued to the game he was playing.

"We've got to decorate the room before Mum gets home," Esme told him.

Alex didn't look very pleased at having to turn off his game. He started arranging Christmas cards on the shelves of the bookcase while Esme unpacked the nativity figures from a box and placed them on the windowsill.

"They don't go like that," said Alex, moving the three wise men to a different position.

"Yes, they do," argued Esme, moving them back.

Alex glared at her. "OK then, fine. If you're doing the nativity figures, I'll get the tinsel and *I'll* decide where that goes."

He stomped to the cupboard under the stairs and Esme heard him rummaging around. Then all of a sudden he gave a shout.

"What is it?" Esme hurried through to the hall and gasped. The carpet was covered with tinsel strands.

"It wasn't *my* fault," protested Alex. "It all fell apart when I took out the box!" He pointed to some holes. "Look, mice, I think."

"Dad!" Esme shouted.

Mr Browne came in and groaned. "I'll get the hoover. Can you two put up some Christmas bunting in the lounge instead?"

Their dad started hoovering but after a few seconds, the hoover started making strange clunking noises.

"Now the hoover's broken!" Mr Browne said in dismay.

"Um … Dad," Alex said. "I can smell burning."

Esme's eyes widened. "The mince pies!"

They all ran into the cluttered kitchen and Dad pulled open the oven door. Esme and Alex started coughing as dark smoke billowed out. The mince pies were completely ruined.

"Everything's going wrong!" Mr Browne said.

"Poor Dad," whispered Esme as she and Alex backed out of the room.

"Let's finish putting up the decorations as quickly as we can and then help him clear up the kitchen," said Alex.

Esme nodded and they went to put up the bunting.

After a few minutes Mr Browne stuck his head round the door. "I'm just going next door to see if I can borrow their hoover."

"OK," said Esme. "Is there some hay anywhere for the nativity scene?"

"Yes, in the shed," her dad said.

Alex and Esme got a torch and went out into the back garden. It was a cold, frosty night and the air stung their cheeks.

As they headed towards the shed, Esme saw a movement in the shadows.

"What's that?" She pulled Alex's arm so the torch shone on the side of the shed. Two eyes stared at them, reflecting green in the torchlight. "Look!" Esme saw a dog's nose, long ears and silky golden fur.

"She's a cocker spaniel."

The dog backed away.

"It's OK, we're not going to hurt you," Alex soothed. He moved the torch so it wasn't shining into the dog's eyes and crouched down. "Come here."

The dog crept towards them, its head low and its tail between its legs. Alex and Esme kneeled down and let the dog sniff their hands, then Esme tickled her under the chin and gently took hold of her collar.

"She's injured," said Alex, pointing at the dog's front leg. There were streaks of blood on her golden fur. "We'd better take her inside."

Esme picked up the dog, who snuggled against her chest, burying her nose in her neck and licking her chin.

"She's very friendly!" she giggled as she carried her into the kitchen.

Alex cleared the kitchen table and put a towel on top so Esme could put the dog down. The spaniel wriggled a little and tried to jump off but Esme held her still, murmuring softly to her.

Alex fetched some water in a bowl so the dog could have a drink, then filled another bowl with freshly boiled water from the kettle. He found some cotton wool and they bathed the wound.

The dog whimpered slightly and licked Esme's hand but she stayed still.

Just as they were patting the wound dry with a clean towel, Mr Browne came back in with next door's hoover. He looked at the dog in surprise. "What's going on?"

Alex and Esme told him what had happened and Esme said, "I don't think the wound's very deep... Can you take a look?"

Mr Browne stroked the spaniel and inspected her leg. "You've done a very good job cleaning it up," he told them. "It's not deep but it could do with a dressing. Let me get my bag."

Fifteen minutes later the wound on the dog's leg had been dressed with a bandage.

The dog didn't have a tag on her collar but Mr Browne checked her microchip and phoned the company to trace her owners.

"All sorted," he said, putting down the phone. "I've spoken to her owner, Mrs Lacey. She's going to come round to pick her up. Sandy's been missing for a few days."

"Sandy. That's a sweet name," said Esme.

Esme and Alex gave Sandy more water and some chicken from the fridge, and made her a bed in a cardboard box. They placed it in front of the fire and she settled down to sleep while they finished decorating the lounge. Meanwhile their dad got on with hoovering and tidying.

"There's not much I can do about the mince pies," he said, coming into the room. "But at least the house is looking more festive now."

"Maybe that's Mum!" said Alex, hearing the sound of a car and jumping to his feet. He rushed to the window. "No," he said. "It's a lady that looks about Gran's age."

"That'll probably be Mrs Lacey, Sandy's owner," said their dad.

Mrs Lacey was slim with short grey hair. As soon as she spotted Sandy, her face lit up. "Sandy!"

The dog whined and held up her injured paw.

Mrs Lacey hurried to the box. "Oh, Sandy, I've been so worried about you!" she said. "Thank you so much for looking after her," she said to Mr Browne, Esme and Alex. "A delivery man left the gate open and she got out two days ago. I was so scared she'd been run over."

"I've checked her over and there's nothing to worry about," said Mr Browne. "Just a small cut on her leg."

"I'm so grateful," Mrs Lacey said as she carried the dog to the car and settled her in her crate. Then she handed Mr Browne a tin. "I bought these as a little thank you – they're just some mince pies I made."

"Thank you – they're actually just what we need," he said, winking at the children.

As Mrs Lacey drove away, they all waved. Esme felt a flicker of sadness at saying goodbye to Sandy but she was glad the little dog had been reunited with her owner.

As they turned to head back inside, Mrs Browne arrived home.

"Hello. What's happening?" she said. She looked tired, with her dark hair escaping from her low bun and a smudge on her face.

"It's a long story," said Mr Browne. "But Esme and Alex have been wonderful this afternoon."

Esme grabbed her mum's hand. "Come inside and we'll tell you all about it!"

They went into the house. When

Mrs Browne walked into the lounge, she stopped in surprise. "Oh, wow! Christmas has arrived!" she said.

"Do you like it, Mum?" Alex asked eagerly.

Mrs Browne smiled. "I do!" She sat down on the sofa. "Now, tell me everything that's been going on."

On Christmas morning, when Esme and Alex went in to wake up their mum and dad, the bedroom was empty.

"They must be up already," said Esme.

They raced downstairs and found Mum in the kitchen.

"Where's Dad?" asked Esme.

Her mum smiled. "He's just popped out – he'll be back soon. But he did say I can let you have the first part of your Christmas present now." She pointed to the kitchen table, where two small parcels sat.

Esme unwrapped hers curiously and found a lead while Alex unwrapped two dog bowls.

"What are these for?" Esme said, her heart beating a little faster.

There was the sound of a car horn outside.

Esme and Alex hurried to the door. Their dad was letting a young golden retriever out of a crate in the back of the car. She had eyes the colour of dark chocolate and a coat as white as a polar bear's.

"What's happening?" Esme swung round and looked at her mum. "Is it…? Is she…?"

Her mum smiled. "Yes, she's for you. For both of you."

Esme and Alex kneeled down and the dog bounded up to them, licking their arms and legs and wagging her plumy white tail.

"She's called Holly," said Mrs Browne.

"She's gorgeous!" breathed Esme, stroking her. "But you said we couldn't have a dog."

"When I saw how good you both were with Sandy, I talked to Mum and we changed our minds," said their dad. "I was really proud of the way you both acted that day. Holly will be your responsibility, though, so you have to promise you'll look after her."

"We promise!" they both said.

"Why don't we all take her for a Christmas walk?" Mrs Browne said.

Holly woofed happily, Alex whooped and Esme flung her arms around her mum.

"Happy Christmas!" Mrs Browne said, with a smile.

THE LEGEND
OF PEMBA

Swapna Haddow

"I'll jump higher than you both," Diki shouted to her brothers.

"I'll jump over you and higher still," her older brother, Tashi, roared back.

The two snow leopard cubs dived through the snow, their grey fur coats now dusted in white, as they leaped over each other and danced from rock to rock in the dusk. Chiri, the youngest of the three cubs, tumbled along after them, racing to keep up with his brother and sister.

Aside from the cubs and their mother, there wasn't another creature for miles.

High up in the Himalayan mountains, far from where the humans lived, the ravines were steep and tricky to climb.

"Ma?" Tashi called to his mother. "Am I the bravest of us three?"

"Just because you're the oldest, it doesn't make you the bravest," Diki said, not wanting to be overlooked. "My Brave is bigger than yours. In the future there will be legends of my Brave, just like the legends of Pemba."

Their mother laughed, nudging along Chiri, who had fallen behind, as the family headed home to their den.

"There won't be legends of Chiri," Tashi whispered to Diki as they watched their younger brother being carried by their mother in her mouth. "He doesn't even have a Brave."

"Tell me about Pemba," Chiri asked his mother, ignoring his siblings. He struggled out of her grip and rolled ahead of the others.

"Pemba was the boldest of snow leopards," Diki said, keen to prove she was the authority on the great snow leopard. "She would venture across the mountains on daring journeys and heroic quests. That's something you would know nothing about, little brother."

"I can be as brave as Pemba," Chiri growled back.

Watching his brother and sister dive from boulder to boulder, Chiri felt his heart race. The icicles hanging from the rocky arches looked like jagged teeth, sharp enough to slice right though him.

But Chiri wanted to prove he had a Brave, too.

Squeezing his eyes shut, he leaped up to join his sister on the snow-covered rocks. As he landed, his paws slipped on the ice. He crashed back into the snow and hurtled down the mountain face, skidding faster and faster.

He couldn't breathe. The air felt frozen in his chest.

He wanted to scream but nothing came out.

It was his Fear.

He tried to squash it down but it rose from the pit of his stomach, gripping his entire body. Spinning out of control, he smashed into a tree, clattering the icicles on the branches.

Chiri cried out and his mother ran to him and scooped him up, wrapping him tightly in her fur. Salty tears streamed down his face and on to his mother's thick coat.

"Nobody will tell stories of Chiri's Fear," Diki laughed.

"That's enough," Ma scolded.

Chiri hid behind his mother's legs, watching Diki and Tashi return to bouncing and soaring over the snow dunes as they talked of the fearless Pemba.

"She was the bravest of *all* the mountain creatures, not just the snow leopards," Diki said. "She could hurdle over canyons."

"I heard she once battled a dragon in the ravines," Tashi agreed.

"I heard it was two," Diki purred. "Pemba found adventures in every cavern."

"I'm not sure *that's* true, my darling," Ma said, herding her cubs into their den.

"That's because *you're* just a ma," Diki said. "You've never had to find your Brave."

Ma laughed. "It's time for bed, little ones."

The sky was now an inky blue, dotted with twinkling stars.

As they snuggled up in their fur-lined den, Diki pulled at her mother's tail. "Tell us a story about Pemba."

"Please?" All three cubs looked up at their mother, their eyes bright and keen.

"OK," Ma said. "But you have to promise to go to sleep afterwards."

"Tell us the story of how Pemba found her Brave," Chiri said.

Ma wrapped herself around the cubs and drew them in close. "This story starts high in the mountains, above the clouds, where snow leopards are the guardians of the range."

"I'll be the best and bravest guardian of them all," Tashi announced.

"No, *I* will be," Diki said. "I'll be just like Pemba."

"Pemba was indeed very brave," Ma continued. "And she had to be."

Ma told of a time when the blizzards were often and the snow was as deep as the oceans. The wind rocked the mountains and the air would turn to ice before your eyes.

"And it was on one night, during the heaviest of the snowstorms, that Pemba had to call on her Brave."

The cubs snuggled closer to their mother, not wanting to miss a minute of the story.

"Why did she need her Brave?" Tashi asked. He stretched out his back legs and his spotted fur rippled.

"Pemba heard a sound on the wind," Ma said. "It was not the sound of a beast. Nor the sound of a bird."

"What was it, Ma?" Chiri asked.

"It was the sound of a man."

The cubs gasped. They knew all about the humans in the villages at the bottom of the mountain, and how the snow leopards and the men stayed away from each other.

"Why was a man in the Leopard Mountains?" Tashi said.

"*That* is exactly what Pemba wondered," Ma replied.

Ma told of how Pemba listened again. And again, heard the sound. It was a cry.

A loud, piercing howl.

The man was scared.

"What did Pemba do?" Diki said.

"She went out into the snow," Ma said. "She followed the sound, through the ravines and through the ice. And even though her chest felt like it was on fire from the freezing air and the snow was stinging her eyes, she continued until she found a small man-cub covered in snow. Pemba saw that the child was not alone. The child was with a man and a woman."

Chiri huddled closer to his mother.

"Pemba must have frightened the man," Ma continued. "The human stood over his child and whipped a branch at the leopard. His Fear made him protective of his cub."

"Was Pemba hurt?" Diki said.

Ma nodded. "The branch caught Pemba's

paw and cut it deep. The snow fell harder and the child cried, scared in the dark. The child's parents held their cub close to them but the child shivered uncontrollably as the cold pierced his bones.

"Though her paw was hurt and her Fear was great, Pemba knew *she* could keep the child warm. She lay down. First by the mother, to show she meant no harm. And then she pulled the man-cub into her fur."

"Was Pemba scared?" Chiri asked.

"Of course she wasn't," Diki said.

"Because she's a defender of the mountains," Tashi said. "She protects all the creatures. Even the men."

"That's right, my cubs," Ma said. "But she was afraid. Her paw stung and the snow felt like hot coal against her injured skin. Still, she wrapped the child in her fur because he needed protection from the storm."

All three cubs stared at their mother, their mouths open in awe.

"The man had understood that Pemba wanted to help," Ma continued. "He wrapped her paw in his scarf and in turn she let the family shelter in her fur. Pemba kept them warm until the final snowflakes fell and the snowstorm had passed."

"She must have had the biggest Brave," Tashi said sleepily.

As the cubs yawned, Ma gently kissed

each of them on the head.

"Pemba protected the family and kept them safe until they were able to journey down the mountain the next morning. A snow leopard leaves no beast, bird or man behind."

As Diki and Tashi drifted off to dream of playing in the snow and jumping ravines, Ma padded to the entrance of the cave and looked out over the mountains.

But Chiri could not find sleep for thinking about the story his mother had told.

He scampered up to Ma as she gazed at the snow beyond the den, deep in her own thoughts. He licked at his mother's paw to get her attention. As he did so, he felt a ridge. He buried his face further into the fur on her paw and that's when he saw it.

There, deep down, was the scar of an old injury cutting across the paw.

Chiri looked up at his mother and he knew.

"Did your Fear come for you when you met the man family?" Chiri asked.

"It did," Ma replied.

"Where did you find your Brave?"

"I didn't have to find my Brave," Ma said. "My Brave found me." She nuzzled the young cub. "Just like your Brave will find you when you need it."

"But my Fear feels so big."

"Being brave doesn't mean you don't have fear," Ma said. "You will find your Brave, my cub."

"But my Fear—"

"Is yours to master," his mother said, smiling at him.

He looked out of the cave and then back at his mother, who nodded him on.

Chiri stepped out of the den. The giant boulder at the entrance of his home was one he had seen his brother and sister jump many times. Chiri had never dared try it himself. His Fear had made sure of that.

In the moonlight, the icy rock loomed over him, casting a dark jagged shadow over the little cub. Chiri felt his body start to tremble. He shook away the thoughts of his fall earlier that day, remembering his mother's words: *Being brave doesn't mean you don't have fear.* Instead of squashing down his Fear, he held on to it, determined to match his Fear with his Brave.

Chiri looked up at the rock, unable to see the top. Then, with a deep breath and his eyes shut tight, he jumped up to the frozen boulder.

He felt the cold air through his fur as he sprang up, reaching towards the rock. As his paws clattered on the ice, he held strong.

He'd done it! He'd landed the jump. He'd found his Brave.

"I did it, Ma! I did it!"

"You did, my sweet cub."

Chiri smiled down at his mother and thought about how even the bravest of leopards had Fear and that it was Fear that helped them find their Brave. He thought about the snow dunes he would jump with Tashi and Diki in the morning. He jumped down from the top of the boulder and skipped over to his mother, where she wrapped him up in her body and held him tight.

Nestled in Ma's warm hug, Chiri listened as she hummed a tune that sounded like the wind dancing through the mountains.